A NOTE TO PARENTS

Young children can be overwhelmed by their emotions--often because they don't understand and can't express what they are feeling. This, in turn, can frustrate parents. How can you help your child deal with a problem if the two of you don't even share a common vocabulary?

Welcome to **HOW I FEEL**--a series of books designed to bridge this communication gap. With simple text, lively illustrations, and an interactive format, each book describes familiar situations to help children recognize a particular emotion. It gives them a vocabulary to talk about what they're feeling, and it offers practical suggestions for dealing with those feelings.

Each time you read this book with your child you can reinforce the message with one of the following activities:

- Ask your child to make up a story about a little boy or girl who is happy.

- Make a list together of happy words--real or imaginary.

- Act out situations that make your child happy, and ways your child can make others happy.

- Encourage your child to express his or her emotions using the **HOW I FEEL** activity card and reusable stickers included with this book.

I hope you both enjoy the **HOW I FEEL** series, and that it will help your child take the first steps toward understanding emotions.

Marcia Leonard

Executive Producers, JOHN CHRISTIANSON and RON BERRY
Art Design, GARY CURRANT
Layout Design, CURRANT DESIGN GROUP and BEST IMPRESSION GRAPHICS

HOW i FEEL

HAPPY

by Marcia Leonard
illustrated by Bartholomew

This little girl is painting a special picture.
She feels happy.

This little boy is happy, too.

He's the first one
to make tracks in the snow.

These kids are happy
just turning somersaults.

Have you ever felt that way?
Can you make a happy face?

This little boy is glad
because he found something
he thought was lost.

Do you have a favorite toy
that makes you happy?

These two kids are best friends.
They feel happy when they're together.

Is there someone you're always
glad to see?

This whole family is having
a wonderful time.

What does your family do
that makes you happy?

Sometimes happiness is
a warm, quiet feeling
that makes you smile.

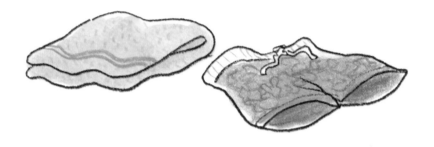

Sometimes it's a bubbly, tickly feeling
that makes you laugh.

You can make yourself happy
by doing things you like to do.

And you can make
other people happy, too.

Happiness is a feeling
you can share.

HOW-I-FEEL
Instructions

Use this How-I-Feel chart to help your child identify and express a variety of emotions. Gently remove the page of reusable stickers from the center of this book. Ask your child to choose the face that matches how he or she is feeling-- right now--and place it on the chart. Then ask your child to choose the face that shows how he or she would *like* to feel, and place that sticker on the chart too. Are the faces the same? Try using the How-I-Feel chart all week and talk about the emotions that the faces express.